To the Seagulls of Tatamagouche,
with love. MR
For Livvy and Elena Curtis. TK

Published in the UK by Scholastic, 2022
1 London Bridge, London, SE1 9BA
Scholastic Ireland, 89E Lagan Road, Dublin Industrial Estate, Glasnevin, Dublin, D11 HP5F

SCHOLASTIC and associated logos are trademarks and/or registered trademarks of Scholastic Inc.

Text © Michelle Robinson, 2022
Illustrations © Tom Knight, 2022

The right of Michelle Robinson and Tom Knight to be identified as the author and illustrator of this work has been asserted by them under the Copyright, Designs and Patents Act 1988.

ISBN 978 0702 31333 2

A CIP catalogue record for this book is available from the British Library.

Printed in Slovakia
Paper made from wood grown in sustainable forests and other controlled sources.

1 3 5 7 9 10 8 6 4 2

This is a work of fiction. Names, characters, places, incidents and dialogues are products of the author's imagination or are used fictitiously.
Any resemblance to actual people, living or dead, events or locales is entirely coincidental.

www.scholastic.co.uk

MR KOOL'S

SCHOLASTIC

WHEN ICE CREAM HAD A MELTDOWN

MICHELLE ROBINSON & TOM KNIGHT

Ice Cream lives inside a van.
It visits lots of places,

spreading joy and sprinkles,
putting smiles on people's faces.

CORNWALL

SCOTLAND

LONDON

Ice Cream and her friends can't wait
to be picked out and chosen!
Making people happy's WAY more fun
than staying frozen.

The first to go is Wafer Top.

Ice Cream says,

I don't mind.

Of course she does mind, really,
she's just super sweet and kind.

Every time a line forms,
Ice Cream's heart fills up
with **hope.**

She watches, waits
and wonders.

Nope.

Orange Juice and
Strawberry split.
Chocolate Sauce
goes, too.

Ice Cream keeps on smiling, but inside she's feeling blue.

Time goes on.
The freezer fills with brand new
friendly faces.

Ice Cream greets them warmly as
they settle in their places.

Next day, all the kids show up and form a
hungry line. Ice Cream's left behind again.
She sniffs and says, "I'm fine."

Sprinkles goes,
then Triple Scoop.
"Goodbye, Ice
Cream! Take care!"
Ice Cream feels upset.
She starts to cry.

It's just not fair!

Perhaps the gull will pick her...?

COR

But it picks fallen fries.

Ice Cream has a

MELTDOWN.

"I will **ALWAYS** be alone!"

The tears drip-drop and dribble down her crunchy, crumbly cone.

The others say, "You'll get picked soon –
you're such a lovely treat.
Take a deep breath. Count to ten.
Stay cool. Stay calm. Stay SWEET."

They dab her with a napkin.
Are their kind words really true?

A little kid approaches. What will happen?!
Wait and see . . .
"That sweet, white, whippy ice cream looks like
just the one for me."

And Ice Cream grins in triumph
as – at last! – she gets her dream.

She waves goodbye to her old friends and hears them shout,

HOORAY!

Each and every ice cream hopes
their tale will end this way.

So, when you choose an ice cream
pick the one that's right for you –
and know that if you're happy
then your ice cream's happy, too!